# COME ON WITH
# THE PUNT

MARCH HARE STORIES

# COME ON WITH
# THE PUNT
## MARCH HARE STORIES

## Paul Dean

PEDLAR PRESS

St. John's

COVER ART John Hofstetter, *Battened Down* (2015, digital photograph)
DESIGN Graham Blair Designs, St. John's NL
TYPEFACES Garamond, Chaparral, Gill Sans
PRINTED IN CANADA Coach House Printing, Toronto

LIBRARY AND ARCHIVES CANADA CATALOGUING IN PUBLICATION
Dean, Paul, 1950-, author
    Come on with the punt : March hare stories / Paul Dean.

ISBN 978-1-897141-74-8 (paperback)

    1. Dean, Paul, 1950- --Childhood and youth. 2. North Harbour (Placentia Bay, N.L.)--Biography. I. Title.

FC2199.N585Z49 2016        971.8        C2015-906661-1

ACKNOWLEDGEMENTS
The Publisher wishes to thank the Canada Council for the Arts and the NL Publishers Assistance Program, for their generous support of our publishing program.

For my four sisters and my brother

For Melvin Stacey and all the crowd from
North Harbour, Placentia Bay

# CONTENTS

The Oldest Fish in Newfoundland     1

Come On With The Punt     8

Melvin     12

The Song That Killed Ern Reid     18

Charl out on the Island     21

'Tis Not for the 'Gard of the 'Cardeen     26

Santa's from the Bight     31

Yesterday for Eric     34

Reading Mother's Diary     39

West Moon in the West Indies     48

Lou Hynes and the Virgin Mary     56

Our Father     62

Acknowledgements     73

# THE OLDEST FISH IN NEWFOUNDLAND

I have discovered something really important, important to me anyhow, and perhaps to the rest of you if you'd stop to think about this like I did. I have figured out the time and circumstance of my conception. This process has led me to the stark conclusion that the moment of conception was the defining moment of my entire life and that all my significant events since that moment have been determined by it.

Figuring out the timing was easy. I was born in the middle of May, 1950, thirteen and a half months after the union of the Dominion of Newfoundland with the Dominion of Canada. Therefore I was conceived four and a half months after this Confederation, just about when my Mother would have received the first "Baby Bonus" cheques for my three sisters. Five dollars a month for each one, which was more than enough to buy clothes and get them ready for school, and more money than Mother made when, at the age of eighteen, she first came from Hay Cove to North Harbour to teach in the one-room school.

It would have been a happy time for her, the middle of August, 1949. Father would have been home, waiting for a message to return to the lumber woods in Millertown or to construction work in

Stephenville. He had just passed his thirtieth birthday that spring. She was twenty–five and knew she was the only woman he had ever loved and would ever chase around a kitchen.

"Let's go berry picking," she said. "It's a nice day and a westerly wind. There'll still be bakeapples on the bogs on the other side of the harbour. The raspberries are probably ripe too. Eileen can look after the girls."

"All right" he replied. "I'll get the motorboat ready. Make us up a lunch. And bring warm clothes and a blanket, in case the wind freshens. It'll be blowing against us coming home."

They landed the motorboat in the cove below Split Sail Point and could still see their house as they looked directly back across the mile-wide harbour they called home. They took their berry buckets in hand, and with the lunch in the knapsack walked the familiar narrow trail from the cove to the bakeapple bogs, only fifteen minutes from the boat.

"There's loads of bakeapples," she shouted. "Some of them are a bit too ripe but we'll have no trouble filling the buckets."

"I brought an extra bucket," he said, "so you won't have to do like Aunt Drucella done last summer when she took off her drawers and tied up the legs and filled 'em full of bakeapples, there was so many."

"Go on Les, she didn't!"

"That's what Uncle Will told me, and I'd say he asked her to do it."

When her bucket was nearly full of bakeapples, she said, "I s'pose we'll have our lunch now. I got some bread and jam and tea and some dried caplin."

"All right, but it's too warm for a fire," he replied. "I got lemon crystal and a bottle of well water in the knapsack. There's a nice dry spot on that knob over there by the edge of the bog."

They didn't talk a lot during the slicing and passing of the bread and the mixing of the lemon crystal and water. She thought what a nice day it was and how safe she felt with this man, her husband of nearly seven years now, who always remembered the things she sometimes forgot or overlooked. He thought how lucky he was to have such a fine woman, so full of life and such a good mother for their three little girls.

He finally spoke. "The girls are coming along all right."

"Yes," she said. "And it's a lot easier with Eileen here from Kingwell to help out."

"Did you ever think we might have another one, Hilda?"

"Well, we don't get much chance to think about it, with those little girls getting in and out of our bed all the time and calling out for a drink of water and always getting up to pee and whatnot."

"That's a fact," he said.

"But," she said, "I always wanted a boy. I even had a name picked out. I'd call him Paul."

"That would be nice," he said as he reached for her arm.

She embraced him, and there on that dry knob on the edge of that bog, they did the deed that men and women must do: had relations, made the animal with the two backs, made out, made love, made me!

The next spring, I was being brought into this world in the back kitchen of their house in North Harbour with Jenny Stacey as the midwife.

"I'll be all right" she said to Jenny. "No one belong to me ever had any trouble having babies, and Grandmother Burton from Haystack delivered hundreds on Long Island with no doctor or nurse heard tell of."

"Well, you got the boy!" Jenny shouted as she helped me into the light of day. "Les will be some pleased."

"*I'm* some pleased," she said. "I'm going to call him Paul."

By September, Mother was back on the berry grounds and I was back to my roots. She would carry me to the berry grounds (partridge-berries this time) in the knapsack on her back, and place me in some little mossy hollow while she picked berries all around me until I was out of sight or until I bawled. I seldom bawled. This was where I belonged! I was warm and comfortable and quite content staring up at the blue sky and the fluffy clouds or a scattered bird or the hem of a flowerdy cotton dress as Mother would come near to move me to another little hollow near a new patch of berries.

When I couldn't see her, I could always hear her as she chatted to Aunt Ann or Aunt Elsie while they picked their way through another summer of berries. When she wasn't talking, she sang: songs, hymns, ditties. It didn't matter to me. I knew she was there and she knew I was safe and content. This was the whole world.

When I learned to walk, I was sent outdoors every day, sometimes with the proper gear on, sometimes in bare feet, depending on which one of my sisters was charged with rigging me out. I often wore my sisters' dresses because that's what they wore and sometimes that's all there was. I eventually learned how to rig myself out and would bolt out of doors to dig in the beach and the sawdust, make dams in the small brooks, pick blueberries in the garden or just lie down in a warm hollow and have a nap.

Father was working away most of the time when I was a young boy and I spent a lot of my days on my own, roaming the hills, climbing cliffs, catching trout and finding new ponds, secret berry patches and birds' nests. I got lost once and they had to come looking for me and didn't find me until long after dark. They were awfully glad to see me, but no one told me not to go anymore, so I kept at it. Sometimes I took along the dog but mostly I was by myself. I spent days and weeks and months like that, like the salmon I suppose, getting back to the place I was spawned.

When I was about fourteen, I learned that there were people called "geologists" who went around looking at rocks, trying to figure out how they came to be formed or if they were good for anything or contained precious metals. Well this was it! Someone can get paid to do what I have been doing since I was a small youngster. I was going to be a geologist!

## 2

After a bunch of summer student jobs, a year on the Mainland, two university degrees, a marriage and a divorce, I landed a full time job with the government of Newfoundland and Labrador as a Senior Geologist. I was thirty. By this time, all of us, including my younger brother and sister, had left North Harbour for education, work and marriage. Mother and Father, having reared all six of us, were also grandparents by then, but found themselves alone in the house they had built and filled with youngsters and joys. They wondered how all this had happened so fast, how in their desire for us to be better educated and have a better life, they were left alone, hoping for one of us to visit for the weekend or telephone with some news they could be a bit proud of and tell their friends about. This is something we can actually do for our parents, besides staying out of jail.

One sunny summer day, I was completing a detailed geological study of the bedrock on the shoreline at Codroy in Western Newfoundland when I recognized fossils in the rocks and soon discovered a complete fossil fish, beautifully preserved in the shale bed. The outline of the fish was spectacular, with its head, tail, dorsal fin and scales embedded in the rock. I gazed in awe for a moment and then realized that I was looking at the first complete fossil fish ever found in Newfoundland, the oldest fish in Newfoundland!

Newfoundland: Land of the Fish, *Talamh an Éisc* for the Irish, *Terras de Bacalhau* for the Portuguese. The land that fed fish to the world for centuries, the place whose history and being is all about fish. And here I was, in the presence of the most ancient ancestor of them all, from the Lower Carboniferous Period, at least three hundred and twenty million years old!

I was sensible enough not to screw this up. I was no paleontologist and did not wish to incur the wrath of those who are. A few notes, a few photographs, a detailed description of the location to forward to the provincial paleontologist, Doug Boyce, and I was on my way feeling quite pleased with my discovery.

Two months later I found myself in downtown St. John's, at The Ship Inn, chatting to Ann Budgell who was then host of the Fishermen's Broadcast on CBC Radio. "Ann," I said (over far too much beer), "we found this really old fossil fish out on the west coast. It's the oldest fish in Newfoundland! It might make an interesting story for the Fishermen's Broadcast."

"Maybe on a slow news day," she replied, sounding very unimpressed.

But about a week later, Ann showed up in my office saying "I've got five minutes on the Broadcast today. Let's do the story on your old fossil fish."

"Great!" I said. "Let's find Doug Boyce. He's the paleontologist who has done all the follow up work and can speak to the important details. He also has a great voice for radio." I scoured the building for Doug but could find no sign of him anywhere. Missing as usual. "Where the hell are you," I thought, "you reincarnation of a trilobite!"

"All right," Ann said. "I have to be back in the studio soon. Why can't you do the interview?" Okay. This was my idea and Doug's details might lose the listener anyhow. We taped ten minutes of interview about where the fossil was found, how old was the fish really, what did it look like, is it related to modern fish and might there be more old fish to be found in Newfoundland. I thought no more of it, cursed Doug Boyce again, went back to The Ship Inn for a beer and didn't bother to listen for the interview even if Ann decided to run it.

Out in North Harbour, Mother was getting ready for supper and faithfully listening to the radio, one of the great comforts in her daily work in her now quiet house. Father was out in the shed sharpening a saw. When he came into the kitchen for supper, Mother exclaimed "Oh, you should have been here! Paul was on the Fishermen's Broadcast. You just missed it!"

"What was he doing on the Fishermen's Broadcast?" he asked.

"Well, he was talking about how he found this really old fish out on the west coast. He said how old it was but I don't remember exactly. I believe he told Ann Budgell that it was 300 million years old."

Well!" Father said. "How many lies do he tell! How many lies do he tell!"

# COME ON WITH THE PUNT

When I was a youngster back in Placentia Bay (and in my dreams I am often a youngster back in Placentia Bay), the most important social event of the year was the Christmas concert. In North Harbour, the Christmas Concert always took place in the United Church school, which consisted of two classrooms separated by folding doors that could be opened up to make one larger room for weddings and concerts. The concert always happened just before Christmas Eve or, lots of years, *on* Christmas Eve unless it was Sunday.

This event was always organized by Miss, the lower grade teacher who was always called Miss, even if she became a Missus, as sometimes happened. In addition to teaching twenty or thirty youngsters every subject, every day, in every grade from primer to grade six, Miss took on this task of getting youngsters, who were too shy to say their names in September, to appear on a stage in front of the whole harbour in December and, in a loud, clear voice, pronouncing every single word and every single th, say a memorized recitation of several rhyming verses proclaiming the joys of Christmas. This was no small chore for Miss or for us youngsters, but we all seemed to rise to the occasion and exceed the expectations of Miss, our parents and each other. Before the event, we would all have struggled through several weeks of embarrassing and uncomfortable after-school practices, learning our parts when we would rather be sliding or skating or throwing snowballs or doing anything else besides exposing our vulnerabilities to each other. We only did this because, first of all, once you were asked to have a part in the Christmas Concert, saying no was not an option. And we each knew that Sandy Claus showed up at the end of it all to give us the only present we were sure of getting for Christmas.

We also knew that the whole harbour would be there, even some of the Pentecosts. And most of all, there was the adult part of the concert to look forward to because we never knew what might happen then. The adults of the harbour had a whole different approach to the concert and their parts in it. No shyness among that crowd. Their creed was "Come big or stay home." To us youngsters, they were bold as brass, big as dogs and twice as saucy. They were loud and brazen, and most of all they came with all the gear, props and strange getups imaginable. None of this modern day Donna Butt summer drama festival stuff. If they were going to sing "Jingle Bells," they were certainly going to get a one horse open sleigh on the stage, and there would be strong words over whether or no they were going to have the horse!

One year, they did "Tickle Cove Pond" and the weighty combination of Tillie Slade and Aunt Edith Stacey as the front and back ends of the mare damn near led to total loss of "Kit on the pond" over the edge of the stage.

Of course, these acts all required some complex stage management, so someone was often sent out in front of the bedsheet curtain to sing a song or say a long recitation while the stage was being rearranged with sleigh, stove, sheep or rodney. Hayward Crann, taking on this role, once got carried away singing "Harbour Le Cou" and "hove 'way his chew" right into the bosom of a biggish

Pentecost-looking woman in the front row. Ab Eddy, home from Corner Brook, laughed about that for the rest of Christmas saying, "'Twas so good as a concert."

Once when I was a very small boy, too young to go to school or have a part in the concert, I was sitting on my father's knee waiting for the stage to be rearranged for the singing of "The Squid Jigging Ground." Behind the curtain a crowd of women, including my mother and Aunt Elsie, were getting rigged off in oilskins and boots and Cape Anns battened down, while others were undoubtedly preparing squid lines and jiggers—and likely squids if there were any in the harbour to be had. From behind the curtain Aunt Elsie was heard to say "I certainly wants to be one of the ones lying down." This got a laugh from the crowd but to me it all seemed to be taking too long a time. I whispered to my father, "What's they doin?" He whispered back, "I s'pose they're getting the punt." After another period of shuffling and whispering in the crowd, the anticipation was just too much for me. I stood up on the chair next to my father and bawled out, "Come on with the punt!"

Well the whole schoolhouse erupted into roars of laughter. This was the funniest thing they had heard all night or, it seemed, for years. My father also seemed to think it was very funny and took my arm as he laughed and looked around at the other men in the crowd. I didn't think it was funny at all but everyone seemed to be happy and smiling and they grabbed on to this somehow. For the rest of the concert, whenever there was a longish pause in the program, somebody would sing out, "Come on with the punt" and everyone would laugh again. Even when the concert was over and Sandy Claus called my name to come forward and get my present, I hesitated for a moment, and there were more shouts of "Come on with the punt."

For weeks later, when I would meet people on the road or at the shop or when people would visit our house, they would always smile or laugh and say, "Come on with the punt." It took me a long while to realize that they were not making fun of me, that they said this with some affection and were just being gently thankful for having been given some joy by a child.

At the Christmas concert the next year and for many years in North Harbour, whenever there was a long uncomfortable pause in the program, somebody was sure to shout out, "Come on with the punt!" Everyone would laugh again and become comfortable again with themselves and each other.

I left North Harbour and my two-room school when I was fifteen and I have lived elsewhere ever since, because of education, circumstance and choice. My father died when I was thirty-five, but my mother was still there, living in our house, the house I was born in. We both took great comfort in that. But I know that I can't live there myself. I have broken the continuity that is necessary to belong to the place where I was born and, every time I go back, I am suddenly fifteen or nine or four. But when I dream, I am often the youngster again, roaming alone on the New Burn Hills, and around Cain's Pond, Frenchman's Meadow, Elijah's Point, Maggie's Garden and Sal's Island. And when in my dreams I am lost in the woods inside of Pad Ryan's Cove, my father often calls to me, saying "Come on now! Come on! Come on with the Punt!"

# MELVIN

1

Melvin left the two-room school at North Harbour in grade eight. He wasn't kicked out; he just gave it up. He quit. I don't know how old he was. I just remember that he was older than the rest of us because he had failed a few grades along the way and had to do them over again, so the rest of us caught up with him. The teacher considered him to be a "slow learner" and a bit of a "hard case," someone who would never make it in the higher grades. For the rest of us in the classroom, from grade six to grade eleven, he was pure genius entertainment. We knew we would miss him a lot when he left.

For us, Melvin was half the fun of going to school. He was different. He was tall and lanky with a full head of black curly hair like Bunga in the grade four geography book. His teeth were half black, he had a slight stoppage in his speech, he had bunions on his feet from walking the two miles to school from his father's house on the other side of Goose Cove. He was a fierce fella for bologna and for cocoa. We made fun of him every day and he made fun of us, and everyone else: teachers, preachers, shopkeepers, neighbours and strangers. We would try to tease him by inventing such things as his mother Jenny might say to him when sending him out the door to walk the two miles to school. "Drink your cocoa tea, Melvin, and eat your bologna meat; you can't walk very fast with those bunions on your feet." Melvin's response was always quick and something like "Go on, ye young fellas is still shittin' yella."

He taunted the teacher with his answers to questions. In the grade six geography exam, in response to the question "What do you understand about the rotation of crops?" Melvin wrote "I understand nothing about the rotation of crops." In Canadian history, when asked "Who was Pontiac?" Melvin replied "That's Roy Gilbert's new car."

But he loved literature and could retell any story in exact detail and recite any poem in its exact entirety. His favourite story poem was "John Gilpin," fifty verses long.

> John Gilpin was a ci ci citizen
> Of credit and renown.
> A train-band captain eke was he,
> Of famous London Town.

Ask Melvin to start a poem, a story or a ballad and he wouldn't stop until the very end.

Melvin's love of stories, rhymes and songs kept us entertained well beyond the classroom. On Friday nights, young fellas and girls would walk in around the bottom of Goose Cove and sit on the wooden rails of the Nook bridge and listen to Melvin. He knew every Pat and Mike joke on the go, every rhyme ever written on a shithouse wall and songs we never heard on the radio. He would sing "Quare Bunga Rye" and "The Pub With No Beer" to us young fellas who didn't even know what a pub was. He had an amazing ability to totally transform popular country songs on the radio by changing just a few words: heartache to hard on, lonely to horny, heart to arse. To our juvenile minds, this was hilarious, and it still is to my still juvenile mind when I think of him launching such new hits as "I'm in the middle of a hard on" or "How can I write on paper what I feel in my arse."

Melvin lived next door to the Gilberts, a large extended family headed by the patriarch Albert, known as Ab, who never worked because he claimed to have a bad arm. Ab would say "Melvin b'y, the arm is some bad today. I can't get 'en above me shoulder. Now yesterday, I could get 'en right above me head, way up there," lifting and waving his arm above his head. Ab always claimed he would have been worth a fortune if that Englishman looking for relations of Sir Humphrey Gilbert hadn't turned around at Come by Chance and come no further. Having listened to Ab's lies and watched Ab's wife and family get into all kinds of colourful schemes and rackets, Melvin sat down one day and composed the Gilbert Alphabet. It included the entire Gilbert clan and anybody they had anything to do with.

A is for Ab with the pain in his arm.
B is for Bill, the brother of Darm.
C is for car, they all likes to use.
D is for Don who goes on the booze.

I used to know all of it one time, but my memory has faded as the Gilberts have faded.

When the resettlement program started, the new people who moved to North Harbour from the islands and the western side of Placentia Bay hauled their houses up into the meadows around Melvin's house and became new neighbours for Melvin, his mother and father and his brothers and sister. One Friday there was a great scandal in the Harbour when one of the new fishermen from Port Anne, a married man himself, ran off with Ivy, the wife of one of Melvin's brothers. The scandalous news went on for a week until the man's unemployment cheque ran out and he had to come home to fill out a new form. Melvin said that Ivy had it too good, that's all.

After that, Melvin left North Harbour and took off for Toronto, like so many Newfoundlanders at that time. He got a job driving taxi in Toronto where he met up with a woman from Trinity Bay and started having youngsters. He always said that he only made enough money to pay his traffic tickets, so after a couple of years he gave it up and came home. He moved into his father's house with his wife and his new youngsters. They were building the oil refinery at Come by Chance at that time and Melvin was determined to land a job. He went in to St. John's to see the Premier, Frank Moores. He had no appointment but waited all day outside Mr. Moores's office. Moores finally agreed to meet this determined fellow at the end of the day. "Well, young man. What can I do for you?" he asked. Melvin replied "You got to get me a job at Come by Chance, sir."

"Even if I could, why should I get you a job any more than any other man, Melvin."

"Well sir," Melvin said, "I got a crowd of youngsters, and the big ones are starting to eat the little ones."

Frank Moores actually got Melvin a job at Come by Chance and he worked there while the oil refinery was being built and stayed on until she closed down after the big Japanese bankruptcy. Like many of the men who lost their jobs, Melvin took off for Western Canada and found work digging the tar sands at Fort McMurray in Northern Alberta. He has been there ever since. I haven't seen him since he left North Harbour but I miss him and still think of him often.

At a cocktail reception at an international mining conference in Toronto, at the Royal York Hotel, I once met the Director of Human Resources for Syncrude, a stunning Norwegian woman called Kjersti. I thought she was beautiful. She thought I was interesting. When she learned that I was from Newfoundland, she became more interested and started telling me what great workers the Newfoundlanders are and how Syncrude could not possibly have built the Alberta Oilsands Project without them. "I really like the way the Newfoundlanders talk," she said, "how they interact with each other in such a jovial manner. They remind me of my own people in northern Norway where I grew up. Sometimes they make me homesick. To me they are hardly like Canadians at all."

At that moment, I knew two things: I loved this woman and I wanted my friend Des Walsh present to hear this. Des still takes it hard that we lost our country to Canada. I then took a chance on a long shot. "Did you ever meet a Newfoundlander called Melvin Stacey?" I asked. "He's from my home."

"Why, yes I did!" she answered. "He is one of our best employees, certainly our best drag line operator. You know those long excavators that cost millions."

"What would a guy like that make?" I asked.

"Oh, he'd make over a hundred thousand a year with overtime. He works lots of overtime because he is so reliable. Whenever we have serious difficulties, we always call out Melvin."

"Not a slow learner?" I said.

"No, no, not at all," she replied, "and the reason I remember him most is that over the years, his sons and daughters have won many of our company scholarships. Melvin would always come to the award ceremonies. That's really how I got to know him and his family. Most of his children have now left Fort McMurray and gone on to university. One of his sons is particularly brilliant and is winning many academic awards at the University of Alberta. But I remember them all as such fine young men and women."

Good thing the big ones didn't eat the little ones, I thought.

"You say Melvin is from your home. You should really come to Fort McMurray and visit him and see our operations."

"Thank you." I said. "I'd love to do just that." Because I can't remember who comes after Roy in the Gilbert Alphabet, but I do remember that

> A is for Ab with the pain in his arm
> B is for Bill, the brother of Darm.
> C is for car, they all likes to use, and
> D is for Don, who went on the booze.

# THE SONG THAT
# KILLED ERN REID

*For Des Walsh*

I know nothing about poetry, no more than the woodbox. I only like the company of poets and the company they attract, but I don't pretend to understand them or their poems. For me, the best poems are songs. And maybe the best songs are poems. Like Johnny Cash's "Give My Love to Rose." What's wrong with that for a poem? Some of my poet friends have written songs, which I have enjoyed and understood. Like Al Pittman's "Rocks of Merasheen" or Des Walsh's "O! Bonaventure." But none of them has ever written anything as powerful as the song that killed Ern Reid.

Ern Reid was sick and dying in his house in Harbour Buffett at the time when resettlement was just talk. Some of the younger crowd would gather for parties in the kitchen of Wes Gregory's house next door. This always turned into long singing sessions that were clearly heard in all the nearby houses, especially Ern Reid's. Ern's wife Lizzie would complain that all this singing was disturbing Ern and was no good anyhow and would drive him to his grave if they kept it up.

One night the young crowd was singing "The Tiny Blue Transistor Radio" again for the second time when one of the women came in to say that Ern was dead.

He bought it for my birthday, just one short year ago,
The tiny blue transistor radio.
We stayed up late and listened to the music soft and low,
On the tiny blue transistor radio.
And the man at the radio station made a special dedication,
To Jimmy and the girl that he loves so.
We kissed each other gently, as we listened so intently,
To the tiny blue transistor radio.

And now just one year later, his love for me is gone.
He's out tonight with his new love I know.
And I just heard them playing, the one we called our song,
On the tiny blue transistor radio.
And the man at the radio station made a special dedication,
To Jimmy and the girl that he loves so.
Her happy eyes are glistening, while my sad heart is listening,
To the tiny blue transistor radio.

From then on, whenever it was sung and heard, that song became
known as "The song that killed Ern Reid."

Three years later they floated Ern's house from Harbour Buffett
to North Harbour and parked it on Goose Cove Island next to
Lizzie's daughter Jane and her husband, Charl, the best fisherman
in North Harbour.

One sunny summer's Saturday, ten years later, the house burned
to the ground. No one could remember the last time a house burned
in North Harbour. I could see it all happening very quickly from
my mother's kitchen window as we were listening to VOCM radio.
And as we watched Father and all the other men pouring buckets

of water on the smoke and ashes of Ern's house, on over the airways came the sweet tones of Connie Smith singing: "He bought it for my birthday, just one short year ago, the tiny blue transistor radio." When the song was over, the fire was over and I said "That's the song that killed Ern Reid."

Not all the older people who moved to North Harbour from the islands of Placentia Bay have died. But many have, including Lizzie Reid, who was brought to Thornlea to be buried where she was born. Mr. George Upshall died chasing sheep he brought from Harbour Buffett and never knew their way home. Bessie Haines from Tack's Beach went upstairs one day and laid down and died. And some just got old quickly while others are nearly forgotten. But in North Harbour and in Arnold's Cove, whenever there are kitchen parties and the singing turns to country songs, which it always does with women around, someone will start singing "He bought it for my birthday, just one short year ago." At that moment there is no doubt whatsoever that somebody is sure to say, "That's the song that killed Ern Reid." And so it did!

# CHARL OUT ON
# THE ISLAND

Goose Cove Island was never truly an island in my time since there was always a road and a small bridge along the low neck of land and beach that connected it to the rest of the community of North Harbour. But in my father's time and in my grandfather's time, Goose Cove Island was an island with each high tide and was certainly an island whenever late summer gales or strong winter storms swept across the Neck, taking fences, boats, sheds and, once, during Hurricane Ione, Walt Gilbert's house.

It was certainly an island when Uncle Hedley Brinston came from Sound Island, further out the Bay, and built the first house and cleared the first land of the green spruce that grew to the water's edge. Since then, Goose Cove Island has been home to the Brinstons and two other families, the Baileys and the Eddys, each with their cleared piece of land, their houses and gardens, their fishing stages and wharves and a few animals. Uncle Hedley Brinston fished in North Harbour with an old punt, a set of oars and a browned canvas sail. He made a living without ever taking the old punt outside the harbour, this very large harbour called North Harbour at the northern end of Placentia Bay. The regular cycle of herring, lobster, salmon and codfish provided for him, his wife, Aunt Ellie, and six youngsters: George, Marcie, Rose, May and the twins, Effie and Charl. Uncle Hedley raised these youngsters through "the hard times" of the nineteen twenties and thirties when there was no money and not a lot of fish. Even when times got better, he believed that "the hard times" would come again so he saved every dollar and was known to have tin cans full of Newfoundland five cent pieces and coppers hid in the corners of his house and stage.

The Brinston daughters eventually married young men in the Harbour and started their own families. Effie married a man from the Southwest Arm of Trinity Bay and learned to speak like the crowd from "Down the Arm" who were always talking about cayrs (cars), styached shyats (starched shirts) and caypet (carpet). The rest of them lived close by, including George and Rose who were next door to each other on the Neck. But Charl stayed with Uncle Hedley and Aunt Ellie on Goose Cove Island in the house he was born in. He started fishing with his father when he was nine or ten and spent every night with his mother and father.

It was sister Rose living on the Neck who dubbed him "Charl out on the island" because brother George had called his third son Charles. Rose had five youngsters herself and made a risin' of bread every day of her married life with her husband Stan, and sang her way through all of it. Because the young fellow, Charlie, was in and out of her house every day, she called him "Young Charl" and her brother became "Charl out on the island."

"Charl out on the island" eventually married Jane Reid who came from Harbour Buffett on the islands further out the Bay and whose father, Ern Reid, was killed by a song. Charl and Jane had two sons, Gerald and Hedley, known as young Hedley. Charl became the best lobster fisherman in North Harbour and did well for himself and his family. He eventually bought an outboard motor for the old punt, but spent very little money except on groceries and school books for his boys. He kept a few sheep, a horse, a few hens, and he would often tame a fox or a crow or a greip.

Charl and Jane lived like this on Goose Cove Island in his father's house well after Uncle Hedley and Aunt Ellie had passed on. Jane had a strong stoppage in her speech, which she overcame by stringing together conjunctions until she was able to get out the intended word. Jane would suggest that they might get a car or a television like the rest of the harbour. She'd say "Charl, the women are all talking about the young and-so-but-the restless, and I don't know what they're talkin' about at all."

Every few years, people in North Harbour would talk about maybe having a town council so that they could have streetlights and garbage collection and such. Charl was always up against this for fear that he would have to give up his "harse." "Besides" he would say, "I got no garbage. What me and Jane don't eat, the hens and sheep will." There is still no council and no debt; Charl still has his harse and there is still no garbage put out by his house on garbage day.

Young Hedley went fishing like his father but the younger son, Gerald, went to Fort McMurray digging the tar sands. Charl keeps hoping he will come home again and build a house nearby or on the land he bought on the other side of Goose Cove. After Charl reached sixty-five and started getting his old age pension, Jane suggested that they should take a trip to visit Gerald. Charl was not tore up on the whole idea. It was not that he couldn't afford to go, but he had never been on an airplane in his life and neither one of them had been west of Gander. Gerald eventually talked him into it, agreeing to meet them in Edmonton so they wouldn't have to change airplanes again.

By the time they actually got to Edmonton, Jane's legs had swole up the size of salt beef tubs and they had to take her off the airplane on the and-so-but-the stretcher. This made it a fairly unpleasant time for Charl, coming and going. When they got back home, sister Rose asked Charl, "How was the trip?" "Well, all right I 'spose" he said. "But I don't think I'll be leavin' the island again."

"What!" she said. "Your first trip outside Newfoundland and you're not going no more?"

"No Rose," he said. "I'm talking about Goose Cove Island. I'm not leavin' Goose Cove Island!"

Sister Rose died last year. She spent six months in the Health Sciences Complex in St. John's and cried every day for someone to take her home. "Take me home, take me home," she would cry to her nieces and nephews when they came to visit. They would reply, "Aunt Rose, we can't take you home. Uncle Stan is dead and there's nobody to look after you." Still she would cry, "No, take me home!" When she finally died and was brought back to North Harbour to be buried, Charl asked the minister if the hearse could take her onto Goose Cove Island before she went to the graveyard. "That's where she wanted to go when she was asking to be took home," he said. So the hearse took her out by Charl's house, where she was born. When it turned around, Charl took his harse and followed the hearse and Rose to the graveyard.

"Charl out on the island" is the last of them now. At eighty-seven, he knows some things he is sure of and some things he is not. After twenty-two years of getting the old age pension from Canada, he knows that "the hard times" are not really coming back, not for him anyway. Jane thinks perhaps they should go into a senior and-so-but-the citizen's home. Charl is sure he's not doing that, and he's not spending no six months dying in no Health Sciences hospital.

Sometimes he thinks he's too crooked to die anyhow. But for now, he's not giving up lobster catchin' as long as he can get aboard the old punt. He's certainly not giving up his sheep or his harse.

And he's not leaving Goose Cove Island.

# 'TIS NOT FOR THE 'GARD
# OF THE 'CARDEEN

*for accordion players quick and dead*

## 1

Back in Placentia Bay, the instrument was variously called a 'cardeen, a cordian, a carjel and, in latter years, the box. It was by far the most outstanding musical instrument of its time in Placentia Bay and all along the coast of Newfoundland. No time was any kind of a time without a dance. No dance was any kind of a dance without an accordion.

The Newfoundland square dance, or set dance, is among the hardest physical activities in the world. Jane Fonda knows nothing about twenty-minute workouts. And athletes who talk of a "runners high" would be hushed by the "high" of the dance in Port Royal or Petit Forte. The "high" was driven by the accordion player, and who was playing for the dance made a big difference to the turnout and the success of the whole event. The crowd and the time and the accordion player combined to create a circumstance wherein cares were forgotten, grudges were settled, women were courted, fantasies were fulfilled and children conceived. A dance often begat a wedding and one wedding was often the makings of another.

Tom Collett caught up with Mac Masters after church one

Sunday morning in Harbour Buffett. "Mac," Tom asked, "will you play for a dance in the Fisherman's Hall next Friday night?"

"No Tom b'y, I can't. Old Wareham wants me to go to Sydney to get a load of coal next week so I won't be back in time. But I got to go over to Port Royal tomorrow. I'll ask Tom Anthony Hann for you."

Mac met Tom Anthony the next day on his wharf in Port Royal. "They wants you to play for the dance in Buffett next Friday. What about it?"

Tom Anthony hesitated. "Well Mac, 'tis all accardin to if you got a good 'cardeen, 'cause if you haven't got a good 'cardeen 'tis all together the other way."

Mac knew exactly what Tom Anthony meant and he also knew what to say to complete his mission. "'Tis not for the 'gard of the 'cardeen b'y; 'tis the 'gard of the man playin' her."

Tom Anthony played his best for the dance in Buffett that Friday and brought a good crowd of Catholics from Port Royal with him. The Hann girls from Port Royal danced with the Wareham boys from Buffett and wondered how they would ever get together with those boys again, they being such Protestants. Tonight could be as close as they would ever get, so close they got. Mac Masters spent that night in the wheelhouse of the Ronald George, in a gale of wind off St. Pierre, singing "Paddy Dover" to himself. And as he finished the last line, "In stormy wintry weather you're not fit to wipe our shoes," he wondered how the dance in Buffett was going, how Tom Anthony was making out, and who was going home with Adelaide Dicks.

Mose Burton, on his way home from the dance, tore every single palin' off Leeland Wareham's fence as he left Harbour Buffett to walk home to Hay Cove, just because it was Wareham's and he had a few drinks of rum in and he didn't go home with Adelaide Dicks or anyone else. Mose always wished he could play the accordion. He even bought one and brought it home to Hay Cove. He always said that he never learned to play it because always after supper, whenever he was ready to start learning, Grandmother Burton would start saying prayers with the first youngster ready to go to bed. By the time she had said prayers with them all, it was time for everyone else to go to bed, including Mose.

Mose had to go through life being known as a bit of a singer on a party. But don't ask him if he can play the accordion. It only makes him mad.

<h1 style="text-align:center">2</h1>

The Harcourt Hotel is a musical landmark in the heart of Dublin, not far from Stephen's Green, "where Miss Henry used to go, sir." The Harcourt Hotel is where every Irish musician of any note has performed and where there is a regular lineup of the best of Irish musicians in one of the most wonderful bars in Dublin. George Bernard Shaw lived at the Harcourt for several years and the restaurant is not only named after him but has Shaw quotations all over the walls. The Harcourt Hotel was where I checked in on May 14, 2000 to discover that the musical lineup that night included Joe Burke, one of the Irish gods of the box, his wife Ann Conroy, also an accomplished player, and Steve Cooney, famous songwriter and master of the guitar. Free admission for hotel guests. At fifty, life does not give better gifts, especially when you are away from home on your own.

That evening while eating my supper in the Shaw Restaurant and reading a Shaw quotation off the wall, in comes Joe Burke, Ann Conroy and Steve Cooney. A quick glance and a soft smile in my direction let me know that Joe Burke knew that I knew who he was. Two hours later, next door, much to the delight of all the guests, especially myself, we were treated to the most amazing and entertaining accordion music. Joe Burke and Ann Conroy both showed their mastery of the instrument. All was pure enjoyment and musical bliss until in comes this Yank, a very good-looking specimen of America with a female of the species in tow. He insisted on making his presence known to all while totally ignoring the music and everything else. I hated him instantly, more than a Bin Laden ever hated a Bush. "Get me another whisky," I thought, while I decide how to kill him. I never felt so mad and alone. I prayed for a buddy like Larry Small or Clyde Rose to be beamed into this. Larry would hate the Yank at least as much as I did and Clyde might go over and explain the finer points of accordion playing, or at least try to steal his woman, which might just distract him enough to shut him up.

Joe Burke finally gave it up and went to a corner table. I felt embarrassed for the whole human race at that moment. I had to get up the nerve to say something to him. I downed another Powers whisky and went over to him and Ann Conroy. "I'm from Newfoundland," I said. "I really enjoyed your playing."

"Jeasus" he said with a smile like Santa Claus. "Do you know Frank Maher?" The world suddenly became whole again as we exchanged stories about Frank Maher, the great player from the Battery in St. John's. Frank Maher, who taught younger players the old tunes and the old style on his single row box and saved Charlie Walsh's accordion from the fire that burned up the Harbour Inn. Frank Maher, who once nervously showed his footwear to an Irish border guard when asked, "What's in your boot?"

In the boot was Frank Maher's accordion.

## 3

In New Bonaventure, Trinity Bay, on New Year's Night, they still have a Newfoundland Square Dance in the Orange Lodge. They have been doing this for the past hundred years or so. Every year the older people say, "This could be the last year for the dance so you better come to this one." This kind of advertising works wonders and they block the place most every year. No liquor is allowed inside the Lodge, but no one cares if you have a box of beer in your truck by the door or a flask of rum in the snowbank. Two or three accordion players spell each other throughout the evening with an occasional appearance by Des Walsh, the fiddle player from Hog's Nose. Women and men in their seventies and eighties, joined by a handful of younger men and women, dance with vigour and with big grins on their faces. They dance very well, shouting "Our side best" and "Round the house!" They only dance like this once a year but never forget the moves. (They're on their own, because Newfoundland set dances go without a caller.) They dance as if their world could end at this very moment and they would be quite content.

The accordion player and the fiddler, who have not met before this January 1st night, are driving the dance but mostly the dancers are driving them. The young perspiring fiddler leans over to the distinguished grey-haired accordion player and says, "No chance of a waltz, I s'pose." The accordion player, without missing a note, leans into his ear and says, "My son, they'd kill us!"

# SANTA'S FROM THE BIGHT

In the millennium year 2000, with my wife Patty and our young daughter and son, Hannah and Stuart, I bought a hundred-year-old house in Trinity East, one of the twelve communities of Trinity Bight that have been, as the highway signs say, "welcoming visitors for 500 years." We were made welcome by people in Trinity East and throughout Trinity Bight, from English Harbour at the north end to New Bonaventure at the south. By visiting the people in their homes and at various parties, and by drinking at Rocky's Bar in Trinity, I became aware of the warmth and generosity and the capacity for fun among this bunch of fellow Newfoundlanders. I liked their banter about each other and some of the more recent newcomers to the Bight, like me and a growing number of others, as tourism activities were taking over from the demise of the fishing industry.

On New Year's Eve, 2005, I was contemplating the pending celebrations over a few beers and listening to Christmas music on the radio. On came the Irish singer Anna McGoldrick, singing a song, "Did Santa Come from Ireland?" Me and the beer thought, "Well that is some foolish song. I can probably write something at least as silly as that!" The result contemplates what the "Santa" of Trinity Bight might be up to at this time of the year as he moves through the geography and the twelve communities of the Bight.

The tune is the same as for Anna's foolish song. It has become my requested "party piece" each Christmas in the Bight.

Did Santa come from Champney's, or maybe Champney's West?
Did he go into the Twine Loft and have a little rest?
Did he pitch out on Fox Island? Did the reindeer get a fright?
If Santa's not from Champney's, he must be from the Bight.

Is he from English Harbour, away out on the point?
Is his workshop out at Horse Chops and does Rudolph keep the light?
Does he call on Dooling's taxi if he gets a little 'tight'?
If he's not from English Harbour, he must be from the Bight.

Is Santa from Port Rexton? Did he walk the Sker-a-wink?
Did he stop at Barbara Doran's house and have a little drink?
Did he spend a night at Fishers' Loft? Did he frighten Frank Lapointe?
If he's not from Port Rexton, he must be from the Bight.

Is Santa Claus from Lockston on the track to Trinity East?
Did he get a big bull moose last fall and have a great big feast?
Does he hang around the trestle when the warden's not in sight?
If Santa's not from Lockston, he must be from the Bight.

Is Santa Claus from Trinity, all in his stocking vamps?
Did he work down at the Shipyard, and have he got his stamps?
I knows he goes to Rocky's 'cause he stays out late at night.
If Santa's not from Trinity, he must be from the Bight.

Is Santa Claus from Dunfield, or maybe from Goose Cove?
Have he got a great big pile of wood to burn in his wood stove?
Did he stop for a scoff at Nan and Pops? Did he pitch out on Fort Point?
If Santa's not from Dunfield, he must be from the Bight.

Is Santa Claus from Trouty where the trouting is so grand?
Did he stop into the Riverside and have some homemade jam?
Did he spin around in Spaniard's Cove? Were the eagles all in flight?
 If Santa's not from Trouty, he must be from the Bight.

Is he from Bonaventure, down at the end of the road?
If you're from Bonaventure, you're either New or Old.
Does he go to the dance in the Orange Lodge most every New Year's night?
If he's not from Bonaventure, he must be from the Bight.

And he stays out late at night. And he gets a little tight.
And you know he's from the Bight!

# YESTERDAY FOR ERIC

The biggest scandal that ever happened in North Harbour in my time was the day that Eric Stacey's wife, Ivy, ran off with Ned Pevie. Pevie had shifted into North Harbour with his wife and family from Port Anne, further out Placentia Bay, under the Resettlement Program. He always said he would never have left Port Anne if it wasn't for the shiftin' money he got from the government. It was enough money to pay the cost of floating his house the forty miles into North Harbour and enough to pay for the small bit of land he needed for the house in the corner of Stacey's garden. Pevie and his family became good neighbours for Eric and Ivy and they got along the best kind, even though they were Anglicans and danced, played cards and had a scattered drink. Eric had recently joined the Pentecosts and believed that the Pevies were sinners, but he did his best to be a good neighbour and helped them out whenever he could. He was even kind enough to help Pevie shore up his house again on Christmas Day after a big square dance with all the Port Anne crowd, dancing until daylight on Christmas Eve, had made it cocksiddle and tilt.

So one day the next fall, Eric got the shock of his life when he came in from fishing and got the news that Ivy and Ned Pevie had run off together that morning to Baine Harbour, where Pevie had a sister they could stay with. Eric had been fishing all that day trying to get his unemployment stamps for the winter, and by the time he got home, his sister, brothers, mother and father all knew what had happened and the word had spread around the whole Harbour. Mrs. Eddy, at the post office, who had helped spread the news, reported that Pevie had got his unemployment cheque early that morning and then took off like a scalded cat.

Eric was in total disbelief! How could this have happened, especially to him? He had done his best to be a good husband to Ivy and a good neighbour to that Anglican sinner Pevie. He couldn't say a word to anyone. He thought about going after them but he was afraid of what he might do or say or what might happen if he actually found them. His sister Ivy, who was always called "Sister Ivy," not to confuse her with Eric's Ivy, said to leave them alone and perhaps they would come back when they came to their senses, or when Pevie's unemployment cheque ran out and he'd have to fill out another form. Sister Ivy was right, as it turned out, but I'm getting ahead of my story.

Eric barred himself in his house and wouldn't talk to anyone. He would need time to think and try to figure out how or why this happened and what he might do next. His mother and father, his brother Tom and Sister Ivy all went in their turn across the garden to try and talk to him but he wouldn't come downstairs or even answer any of them.

Later that evening, the youngest brother, Melvin, who the rest of the Harbour thought of as being the foolish one, spoke up and said to his anxious mother Jenny, "Mother, give me a loaf of bread and a few slices of bologna. Eric is starving over there by now." Jenny knew that Melvin wasn't foolish; you just had to watch what you said around him. So she gave him the bread and bologna and two cups of tea and watched him walk across the garden to Eric's house.

Melvin bawled out to Eric as he put his shoulder to the door.

"Eric, get up b'y and have something to eat. I got hot tea and some bologna for ya." Eric slowly got up and came downstairs. He had a sip of tea while Melvin fried up the bologna on the wood stove. He finally spoke. "Thanks Melvin b'y. I s'pose you heard the news."

"Yes b'y," Melvin replied. "Ivy had it too good, that's all. She had everything from a baby fart to a clap of thunder."

"I don't know about that, Melvin b'y. I knows I'm some up sot over it all. I'm right low-minded. 'Tis like a anchor hanging off of me."

"Was there something you said, Eric, or done to her, that might have got her vexed or anything like that?" Melvin asked.

"No b'y," Eric said. "I've been thinking a lot about that. I might have said something about her soggy doughboys last week, but it wasn't the first time I said that. Now I wasn't very good company for her lately because the summer complaint is on the go and I got a bad case of the cramps."

"We all got that, Eric b'y," Melvin replied. "Mother had to go to Come by Chance to get something for hers, 'twas so bad. I'm sure that wasn't it. What about Pevie? I never seen that much in him. He's no Albert Presley. Was he hanging around much?"

"No b'y," Eric said, "but he had his stamps, I'll give him that. And he could dance. Ivy always said she wouldn't mind going to a dance with them Anglicans. Perhaps I should have thought about that a bit more and gone with her."

Melvin paused a while and finally spoke again. "So he could dance and he had his stamps and you had the cramps! There's got to be more to the story that that, Eric b'y. I'd say it was whatever you said about her doughboys that done it."

"'Tis a job to say, Melvin b'y. 'Tis a job to say. I hope I don't have to shift away myself before this is all over. I'm still so up sot, like I'm in the middle of one of them mournful country songs you hears on the radio. But 'twas good to talk to you, Melvin b'y, 'twas good to talk to you."

Melvin left and walked back across the garden to his mother's house and told them that Eric was all right, a bit low-minded but he wasn't going to make away with himself or anything like that. He laid down on the kitchen day bed and thought about it all for a spell. He kept thinking about Eric feeling like he was in the middle of a sad country song. So he decided he would write a song for Eric. But it wouldn't be one of them mournful country songs. It would be more modern, something like the Beatles. He would sleep on it.

So the next morning, Melvin sat down at his mother's kitchen table and with some of Eric's words and some of his own words and some words from Paul McCartney, he wrote "Yesterday For Eric."

"Yesterday, yesterday. All me troubles seemed so far away.
Now I 'lows they're here to stay, I dare say.
She took off with buddy from out the Bay,
Yesterday.

Suddenly I'm not half the feller I used to be.
I'm right low-minded now you see.
There's a anchor hanging off of me,
Since yesterday.

I haven't got a word to say.
I need a place to hide away.
Perhaps I'll have to shift to Fortune Bay,
After yesterday.

Why she had to go b'ys, I don't know b'ys, 'tis a job to say.
I said something about her doughboys,
Now you know b'ys, not a smart thing to say,
Yesterday.

Now I know that buddy had his stamps.
And I never took her to a dance.
She never hung around with Anglicans
Until Yesterday.

Perhaps I should have gone to Come by Chance,
And got something for the cramps.
Now I know I'll have to change my pants
After yesterday.

Why she had to go b'ys, I don't know b'ys, 'tis a job to say.
I said something about her doughboys,
Which you know b'ys, wasn't right to say
Any day,
Especially Yesterday.

Ivy and Pevie eventually came back to North Harbour when his unemployment cheque ran out, just like sister Ivy said. Eric and Ivy got back together and stayed back together. It had nothing to do with her doughboys after all. Melvin's song was never much of a hit with Eric, so he never sang it much after that.

# READING MOTHER'S DIARY

Our mother died suddenly at the age of eighty-one in North Harbour the week after the March Hare in 2005. My four sisters and I immediately left our own homes in St. John's and Shoal Harbour and gathered at the North Harbour house, the house in which we were all raised and where we knew her best. We dealt with our grief as best we could and shared the loss with our large extended family and close friends in the harbour. We knew it would take some time for this new reality to establish itself within our respective lives, now without her who was so dear to us. We agreed to keep the house as a refuge for all of us and to leave it exactly as it was until we could better deal with it, our home, without her in it.

More than a year later, my sisters decided that it was time to make a start and go through Mother's clothing and personal effects. During this process, my sister Rosanne discovered an old faded, handwritten notebook in the corner of one of the bureau drawers. Upon reading a few pages, she realized it to be a diary written by our mother when she was living with her own family in the tiny community of Hay Cove on Long Island further out in Placentia Bay. This was a diary we had never seen, written before any of us existed, before Mother ever came to North Harbour; before she met our father, now long gone, having died twenty years ago, too early, at sixty-six; before she knew she would be a teacher and a mother; before she knew there would be the six of us. She was a young girl then, fifteen years old, living with her own parents, her four brothers and three other families, all Burtons, in one of the smallest communities in all of Newfoundland with no church and no school.

In the diary she is in grade nine, walking the two and a half miles to school in Harbour Buffett every day and to church there on Sunday, sometimes twice a day unless the family went the three miles to Kingwell. She is getting interested in books and boys. Her closest friend and neighbour is Eliza, daughter of Mr. Will Burton. Her brothers in Hay Cove are Mose, Heber (Heb), Fred and Berkley. Her oldest brother Tom, her sisters Lil, Triffie and Elsie are working away or getting married. The three mothers in Hay Cove are all called Annie so they are called by their husband's names, Mrs. Will, Mrs. Brit and her mother, Mrs. Frank. Uncle Heber, her father's older brother, is a widower and owns the only radio, the source of news about the war that darkens what should be some of the brightest years of her life. She is called Hilda.

Since it was first discovered, we have shared Mother's diary around between the six of us. My sister Brenda has it at her house for safekeeping. I have transcribed the whole diary by hand. It is now my most important means of recalling her presence, particularly when I return to Hay Cove for a week each summer.

Besides each other, Mother's teenage diary is perhaps the most precious gift she has left us. And she did not intend to leave it, no more than she intended her son to read parts of it, first privately, then later, in public, at The March Hare.

Aug. 31, 1939

Eliza and I went out around the beach this morning getting some white rocks for the graves. We went up after dinner fixing them, Eliza and I and Mr. Will. After we had them fixed we went out to Buffett. Eliza had ten cents worth of biscuits and I had some candy. After tea I went over to Mrs. Wills'. Jack Dicks and Wallace are down here tonight [from Harbour Buffett].

This is a lovely night. The hay is mown and the moon is shining on the meadow. I am here in my bedroom and I can hear the sea sighing in the trees. The smell of hay comes through my open window. This beautiful little land set all around by silver hills and little brooks that babble and dance along the hills. They call to me. They cry to me from out their narrow way.

There is talks of war again now.

Signed Hilda Burton


Sept. 1

This morning I worked all the morning. After dinner I went out all the evening. When I came back, I heard war was started. I was terrified. It is between the Germans and the Poles. The British gave the Germans eight hours to withdraw their troops. I suppose tomorrow we will hear the English have joined.

This is a lovely night. I was over to Mrs. Wills' after tea. This is Heb's birthday. He is 19. I wonder where he will be this time next year.

Signed H. B.


Jan 12, 1940

I am starting to write again. I can't write down all that happened since I wrote last. There is so much. The war is still on and many great fights and battles have been fought. Herb Hollett [Tickles] and Les Wareham [Kingwell] went. Herb did not pass [the medical exam].

Uncle Heber has a radio. He got it sometime in the fall. Tom is bringing troops from Canada to England. Lil is married. She married a teacher belongs to Bell Island, John Brown. She is still going on teaching. Triff was home this summer. She is a cook in Queen's College. Elsie is home. She is going to be married in North Harbour. Heb and the rest of us go to school. School is the same as ever. Margaret [Uncle Heber's daughter] is teaching in Bay Bulls.

All the boys in the cove have their names sent in for the Forestry [overseas]. They did not get any word yet. Last night I was listening over the radio to the concert the naval recruits had at St. John's. They sang many old favourite songs. They sang "We will never let the old flag fall." It gave me such a chill to think that I belonged to a country which bore young men so brave as these, willing to give up their life for their country and God.

But I think this was a true saying that Lord Tennyson (or Lord Macaulay) said when he said "How can man die better than facing fearful odds, for the ashes of his father and the temple of his Gods." Fred just came in and he said that The Dazzle was sunk, the schooner that Captain Johnny Murphy is in. They were taken in by a Norwegian vessel.

Yesterday, there were two German ships and two British ships went down. There was also a heavy battle in the air.

This is a dull day. I am going to church tonight I expect. The wind is in the easterd today but it is still bright and cheerful.

Signed  Hilda Audrey Burton

January 23, 1940

I never went to school today. The steamer came [to Harbour Buffett] about one o'clock. Elsie and Daddy went to North Harbour for her wedding. Mr. Brit is down to Uncle Hebers' now.

I enjoyed my walk down [from Buffett] although it was blowing and drifting. I could think of such beautiful things passing through the snowdrifts. I often try to compose things about the beauty of the earth but I think I will fail. It has been one of my greatest dreams to be able to compose verse especially on Nature.

This is a perfect night—a night left aside from Eden as I once read in a book. I can't describe what things look like out of doors. The land is bathed in sheer delight. The moon is sending out its beautiful rays on the snow covered valleys. The spruce clad hills are arrayed in white. The hearts of frost fairies are gay tonight.

I will set out a little picture of Hay Cove to show its beauty, the prettiest place in the world.

Four big homey houses facing each other, a few big trees here and there casting shadows over the snow, a valley nearly level all over with snow. The snow king with his fairies has done his work. Big spruce hills surrounding half of the cove. The moon casting its beams through the trees onto the loaves of the snow. A long beach and beyond the beach a beautiful blue sea, the moon beams making the little waves sparkle like jewels and then as I look to the end of the sea, a wide stretch of blue sea and white ribbon which is not cut exactly fair but in a few swerves and bunches ... and above it all to best beauty is a clear cloudless sky, with very few stars which shine like dew drops on early morning and a beautiful golden moon which will light many happy walkers, wandering lovers and travellers safe to their homes tonight.

March 22, 1940

Today is Good Friday. I did not go up to church today for 11 o'clock service. Don Slade (Elsie's husband) is up from North Harbour. He was over here today. I am going down there this summer. If it is as good as Don says it is, it must be like heaven.

I was up to church tonight. It is a perfect night—a beautiful moon. I enjoyed my walk down tonight. Wallace Dicks came down. He asked me to the time they are having Tuesday night. The CEAA [Church of England Assistant Association] are asking all the fellows that enlisted including the Kingwell fellows. It was very good of them.

Signed Hilda

April 11 and 12, 1940

I shall always remember these past two days to the day I die. I was up to school Thursday. In the night Lew [Burton] came in and said nine fellows were called up. They were going tomorrow. There was a dance in Buffett and we all went up. The fellows who were called up were Mose [Hilda's brother], Lew Burton, Clev Wareham, Frank Dicks, Tom Dicks, Howard Dicks, Angus Hayes, Hector Dicks and Hector Trowbridge.

They were all asked down to Mr. Frank Wareham's to tea. I went down with Mose and had a grand time down there. I did not enjoy the dance very much.

I did not go to school the next day. I went up to Buffett when Mose went. When I got up there Wallace Dicks was going. Frank Dicks was not home and he took his place. They were all going up in the Miss Rita and they could not get her to go, so we walked about the road talking to whoever we met. Wallace told me he would write me but I don't expect he will.

There was a big crowd there to see them off. I shook hands with them all. This has been the hardest day I ever felt pass over me. I hope God will bless them and keep them and send them back to us.

Signed  Hilda

April 13, 1940

Today is Saturday. I went to school because there was nothing else to do. The house is just the same as if someone was dead. I was over to Mrs. Wills after tea. How funny do it seem without Lew. The last time I was over there, Lew came back with me. It was so dark.

Today is a beautiful day. The May flowers are up. I wonder how can Spring come this year.

There were some heavy battles off Norway—7 German ships sunk today, about 1000 men. The British are doing good out there, 18 German ships sunk Tuesday.

This is not a very cheerful place now but we got to keep up our spirits and keep faith.

Signed  Hilda B

April 14, 1940

Today is Sunday and it's some lonesome without Mose. I did not go to church this morning. I went to Sunday school and went out to Uncle John's [in the Tickles] to my tea.

There was a good many tears shed in church tonight. Jack Dicks had to go out and Mrs. Ingram.

Eliza and I went nearly the whole way down to Hay Cove and when I came home I broke down, although I braced up again and wrote to Elsie.

This is a beautiful day but it rained tonight. Rain makes things sadder than they really are.

Signed H

April 20, 1940

Today is Saturday, a beautiful windy April day. I worked all day today. Tonight I went down to Uncle Heber's [to listen to the radio]. There were seven German ships and three aeroplanes shot down. The British are doing good stuff but Italy is going to join Germany. This will make the war long and hard. If the British could keep their navy in Norway, the war might soon be over, but now if Italy joins, that will end it all. The British will not give up to the end.

This is a beautiful night. Everything seems so lonely and everything is waking up after the winter. If only this war had never started. We had such a wonderful summer planned. I will soon be 16, the best years of my life.

I wonder where Mose and Lew are tonight. I pity poor Fred, he misses Mose so much.

Signed Hilda


May 13, 1940

Today is my birthday. I am 16. I often wondered if I would ever be sixteen, and here I am with nothing very much done in this world.

Myrt Dicks gave me a lovely box of stationery. God love her.

It rained all day today. I was up to school. Today we got the reports. I passed with good marks and so did Heb. The Germans are still advancing into Belgium. They can hear the guns in the south of England today. There was a British patrol boat sunk today. Some of the crew were swimming in the water and the Germans fired guns at them.

There are 100,000 Dutch killed, a million men killed now altogether. I am writing this in the kitchen and I suppose we are in the safest place in the world. But over there in Holland, does the line still hold good.

Signed Hilda

The safest place in the world, so far from the war, though its effects reached all the way to Hay Cove, Harbour Buffett and North Harbour, some of the world's most beautiful places. We are all thankful that so many good and loving post-war years were given to our mother, and to us.

# WEST MOON IN THE WEST INDIES

*To the Memory of Al Pittman*

## 1

It is nearly thirty years ago now since our friend Al Pittman decided that he would take part of his sabbatical year with his young family in the southern Caribbean island of Tobago to finish writing *West Moon*, his play based on the resettlement of communities in Placentia Bay. When he announced his plans to his friends in Corner Brook and St. John's, we all said "Great, Al. We'll go to see you." Up speaks one, "Well I'll go." Another one says, "I'll go." "I'll go," says another. Al said "Now b'ys, you can't all go, or at least you can't all go at the same time. There'll be Marilee and me and Kyran and Emily in a small two room place on the lower level of a house in a small village. There won't be much room, as much as I'd like to see all of you." We all said, "Shag it, Al. We can sleep on the beach; it'll be eighty degrees. We're going anyhow!"

I was the only one who went. I went because I found myself in the middle of a miserable February of a miserable winter. I went because I had just made a thousand dollars staking mining claims for Lew Murphy. And I went because I had a marriage that was going on the rocks and I didn't know what to do about it, didn't know whether I wanted to do anything about it, didn't know whether this wasn't a big mistake trying to correct itself. I was twenty-nine and needed to talk to a good friend. Al was thirty-nine and wiser. No better friend to talk to about this, no better person to give advice to heed, no better place to get it.

A quick booking with Air Canada; a hasty visit with Clyde Rose at Breakwater Books to get Al's address and pick up his mail; a brief telegram to Al informing him of my arrival time; a hasty packing of shorts and snorkelling gear and a farewell embrace with Wendy and I was on my way.

I left St. John's in a snowstorm, spent the night on a bench in Toronto Airport, and took off the next morning in another snowstorm, bound for Port of Spain in Trinidad. Food and drink were free on Air Canada then so I asked for a drink of rum. The stewardess brought me two miniature bottles of Newfoundland Screech. Imagine that! Air Canada serving Newfoundland Screech as the rum of choice on a flight to the West Indies! "Could you bring me a few extra, if you can?" I asked. "I'm going to see a friend who would enjoy sharing a few of those."

Late that afternoon, I was on a much smaller aircraft, "The Hummingbird," for the short flight from Trinidad to the smaller island of Tobago. It was eighty degrees. I landed at the airport to see Al on the tarmac jumping into the air and waving wildly, standing out from the small crowd with his black beard and sleek black long hair, looking tanned and as healthy as I had ever seen him. He let out a giant shout of welcome, followed by a bear hug, joyous laughter and a happy introduction to his friends Brian and Inches, young Tobago men whom he had befriended since arriving in November. They had borrowed a car so that Al could be at the airport to meet his friend.

They got us safely back to the village of Plymouth on the north side of Tobago where they all lived with their families. I was received like a lost brother by Marilee and the girls. Emily, who was five, and Kyran, who was ten, welcomed me into their small apartment and balcony on the back of the white concrete house surrounded by tropical vegetation with tall palm trees swaying in the warm breeze overhead. Already, it felt wonderful!

We ate, drank and laughed through the night together outdoors on the balcony. We drank all the Air Canada Screech and Al's rum and sang together into the tropical night. We sang "The Ryans and the Pittmans," we sang "The Badger Drive," we sang "Jack Tar" and "John Kanaka," we sang "Lovely Mary Ann," we sang "Bird on a Wire" and we sang "The Rocks of Merasheen." We laughed and told stories of each other and our mutual friends and sang some more.

The next morning neighbours dropped by to say "Hello" and look me over. They would say, "Oh, Mister Pittman! It is so good your brother has come! He looks so much like you with the black beard and the black curly hair. And your singing! Last night we heard your singing. It was so sad! You must miss your home to be singing such sad songs. You should sing happy songs! Your brother has come!" Kyran and Emily had already discovered their favourite places and delighted in showing me around all of them. They would take to the beach just across the road and collect coconuts for their father to crack open with his machete. They would walk me around the low cliff tops near Lovers Retreat and find stone arrowheads from the old Carib Indian campsites. I would show them volcanic lavas and coral reefs in the coastal cliffs from the time before the island emerged from the sea to become land. We developed our own relationships and became comfortable with each other in our shared closeness.

But my arrival had clearly disrupted the productive routine which Marilee and Al had established for themselves and their family, where Al would write in a secluded corner while Marilee would teach Kyran and Emily their school work for part of each day. Through this well-established discipline, Al had nearly achieved his objective of completing his play and now wanted it to be finished and polished to his satisfaction.

"What can I do, Al, to be more useful?" I asked one day.

"I want you to read *West Moon*," he replied.

"I know nothing about writing plays, Al b'y."

"I'm not asking you to write it! I want you to read it. You know about Placentia Bay and resettlement. You know how people talk and how they say things. I need to know that it sounds right. So tell me what you think."

So I started reading various parts of his play and making a few timid suggestions to Al. I repeated this several times and with each reading got more intrigued with *West Moon* and its characters.

"That one, Rose in the Bed, is a strange character. Where did you dream her up?" I asked him.

"I didn't," he said. "She was my mother's Great Aunt Anastasia from St. Leonard's. She went to bed as a young woman and stayed there. She was "Staish in the Bed" to my mother and them. It's my mother's story more than mine. I just borrowed her for the play."

Within a few more days, on his small portable typewriter on the balcony, Al had banged out another revised draft. We both sat down and read it together word for word. We agreed that it did sound right but I thought it might pose some challenges on a stage production since all of the characters are actually dead. "This might never make it to a stage" he said. "Let's go to Miss Mary's and think more about that."

Miss Mary's was a Tobago Rum Shop in the centre of the village of Plymouth and an easy walk. It was about the size of a good Newfoundland kitchen, three small square tables with low chairs and with Miss Mary, a big, friendly Tobago woman dressed in white, always present in her roles as hostess, proprietor, waitress and cashier. Rum was four dollars a bottle and was to be consumed in the shop. Miss Mary would bring the bottle with as many glasses as there were people at the table. It was Al's favourite place to drink and Miss Mary never questioned his preference for rum. Most white people and tourists in Tobago did not drink rum. It was a status thing to drink scotch whisky and offer a drink of scotch. Rum was considered too common and cheap.

One afternoon, Al was in Miss Mary's drinking Old Oak rum and quietly rewriting the narration part of his play. The only other person besides Miss Mary was an old sailor known as Jacob, having a half bottle for two dollars. He looked at this curious hairy white man drinking rum, and finally spoke to him.

"Where you from, man?"

Al looked up and said, "I'm from Canada."

"Don't know that place, man."

Al went back to his writing and his rum when Jacob spoke again. "You like rum, man. Where you belong?"

"I belong to Newfoundland" Al replied. "It's an island in the North, a long ways from here."

The old sailor suddenly came to life. "Newfoundland!" he exclaimed. "Newfoundland! Why you not say so? What this Canada shit, man? Newfoundland! Fish, man! Salt fish! You drink rum. We send you good rum, man! Why you send us bad fish? Why you send us bad salt fish?"

Al tried to tell him that poorer quality fish, the poorest cull of the sun-dried salt fish from Newfoundland was called 'West Indie' because it was well known that the people of the West Indies were poorer and could not afford the higher quality fish such as the Madeira sent to Spain and Portugal. Like the quality of salt fish that Jack Leonard, the fisherman in *West Moon*, was delivering to Alberto Wareham on the best day of his life. He also tried to tell Jacob that the Canadian Salt Fish Corporation had taken over the marketing of all the salt fish from Newfoundland and most of the fishermen had given up making salt codfish because it was now easier to sell it fresh or directly out of the fishing boats to Russian factory ships.

The old sailor tried to take all this in and then spoke, "Don't know that stuff, man. One time, good salt fish from Newfoundland, big fish, very good fish. Now bad fish, small fish, bits of fish. No good, man. No good at all!"

Within walking distance of the village of Plymouth there are beachside resort hotels that cater to tourists. By Tobago law, they are also open to non-residents and local people. The beaches are all public. The pools, the bars and the restaurants are all outdoors and accessible to everyone. In the tropical evenings, local musicians play calypso in steel drum bands consisting of ten to fifteen people playing on various sizes of polished steel oil drums. The beat is terrific, the sound is amazing and the performance is spectacular. On Saturday night, Marilee and I would go to the Turtle Beach Resort and dance to the steel drum band, drink rum punch, swim, talk and stroll home by the beaches and footpaths, often to find Al still writing or reading. The conversation would then start again and go on late into the tropical night. We talked about our families and friends, our relationships and my troubled marriage.

Al was determined that there was a future for Wendy and I and would encourage me to hang on, to work at it, not to let go of it all. He would say, "It will be too painful for you, too messy, and it will take you too long to recover." Marilee always had a different perspective and was less insistent and, to my mind at the time, more helpful. She was more willing to help me see the inevitable and ponder the importance of letting go gently if that was where I was ultimately headed. They both helped with their listening and advice, and when I was ready to leave them, I knew there was a decision to be made, knew I would be ready for it though still without knowing what that decision would be. This was a decision two people would have to make. I headed home.

## 2

Al and Marilee, Kyran and Emily left Tobago two weeks later and made their way home to Corner Brook after a stop in New Brunswick to visit Marilee's family. Their house in Corner Brook was still rented so they stayed with friends for a while until Marilee got tired of it and checked into the Glynmill Inn, invited all her friends and celebrated her thirty-seventh birthday. She said it was the best birthday she ever had. She thought about going to law school.

Wendy and I decided to let go gently. We made our last meal of a feed of Placentia Bay lobsters, made love for the last time, and said our farewells believing that we were saving two lives. She returned to Toronto. I bought a house in St. John's and eventually got a job. I decided to stay.

Al stayed at my place in St. John's several times that spring and summer, once to help celebrate my thirtieth birthday and more times to get *West Moon* produced on stage. His play premiered on October 31 that year at the LSPU hall, with the graveyard set designed by Gerry Squires, Clyde Rose as the narrator, Pat Byrne as

Bill Sullivan and the rest of Al's close friends in the audience and at the celebration at The Ship Inn after the show.

*West Moon* has been performed many times since then, nationally and internationally, and is now studied in our schools and universities. Each performance and reading is a momentous occasion for Al's friends who knew him so well, and we always go. And we also go to Corner Brook each year for the gathering that is The March Hare, with a core of the same group of friends who read, worked and celebrated with him in the *West Moon* of nearly thirty years ago. We each go for our own reasons, now that he is no longer there, with our own expectations as we grow older and our beards get greyer and our hair shorter. We go because, like the Wind and the West Moon, we have elected to stay. And we go because we believe the words Al wrote on a warm February evening in the West Indies nearly thirty years ago: "In all of times turning, it may not matter that the dead are dead, as long as the living live and remember."

# LOU HYNES AND THE VIRGIN MARY

He used to say that he only took me in because I looked so pitiful when I came to his door looking for a boarding house that summer of 1974. I was just a young fellow returning to university to try and get a Master's degree in Geology and Professor Strong had sent me out to study and map the bedrock of the Fortune Harbour Peninsula in Notre Dame Bay. Lou Hynes was a strong, seasoned fisherman, head of a large family, a storyteller and entertainer. It turned out to be the best summer of my life.

The sun shone every day and there was no wind to speak of until the latter part of August. The rocks were spectacular and spoke easily to reveal the history and secrets of their formation from underwater volcanoes 480 million years ago. The lead/zinc mine in Buchans was on strike, so many of the miners, drillers, hoistmen and muckers returned to their family homes in Fortune Harbour to enjoy the summer on the surface, catch a few codfish, drink beer and write songs for the workers on the picket line.

I hired Lou's son Leo as my boatman to transport me around the coastline and headlands of Notre Dame Bay in his old skiff with the six horsepower Acadia engine. Leo was a diamond driller in

Buchans and was happy to have an extra few dollars for beer and grub. His mother and father were happy enough to have Leo out of the house in the daytime and were more than curious about where we went each day and what I was really up to.

"Now what is it they calls you, going around looking at rocks and stuff?" Lou asked one night after supper. "I am a geologist, Mr. Hynes," I replied. "A GEE ologist! Well Great Jehover! I've heard it all now! Last summer, there was a fella here looking at the landwash, the killop and snails and shore crabs and stuff like that. He said that he was a B'yologist! And he had this young maiden going around with him, giving him a hand and whatnot. I s'pose now she was a Girlologist! You should have one of them with you for company and to give you a hand. She'd be better looking than Leo and not half so hard on beer and grub. You should get one of them for sure!"

During the days when Leo and I were investigating the pillow lavas along the coastline, Skipper Lou and his son Alonzo (Lons) handlined for cod off the near headlands and offshore sunkers. We often joined them alongside their skiff for a lunch of fisherman's brewis cooked up on a fire in a metal tub on boards over the midship room. Lou would tell us of his younger days fishing with Peter Penton out of Fogo Island and his times on the French Shore, the Fischot Islands, Boutitou and Ha Ha Bay. He knew that the inshore fishery was dying and the lifestyle that he knew so well was going rapidly. Still he was full of joy on the water with his son and companion, Lons. They were of the same spirit and never had a cross word except for complaints about small catches and too many jeezly sculpins.

Returning from the fishing and the cleaning and salting of cod, Lou often entered his own kitchen in the late afternoon to find his wife Helen watching television. "What are you watchin', old woman?" he would often say. "I'm watching *Another World*," she'd reply. "Another World, is it! If he's no better than this one, turn 'en off, while we haves a cup of tea. Is Leo and the young rock fella back yet? What's for supper?"

After supper in the long summer evenings, we would move to the large back porch and drink Dominion ale, smoke cigarettes and tell stories. We never turned on a light and often I could only see his bright blue eyes by the light of the cigarette in his mouth. He would tell me all about the French Shore where he said he was born, his winters in the lumber woods, the long walks to Botwood to catch the A.N.D Company train to Millertown and Lake Ambrose. He would often offer his views on the changes going on in the Harbour: the hippies moving into the old houses up in the bottom, the crowd on welfare and the ones getting the 'foolish money.' "They're not so foolish, ya know, that crowd. They got it a lot better than I do!"

He would also talk about losing his closest brother Will by breaking through the ice and drowning, and holding his seven year old son Louis in his arms, dying from being crushed by a falling tree while Lou was cutting firewood. He now feared for his daughter Elizabeth, forty and suffering from cancer. He prayed each day to St. Anne and the Virgin Mary to help her and keep him from losing another one of his children. "A man should not have to suffer that twice in one lifetime," he often said.

Late one night in the back porch, he said, "We're not really Hynses, you know. Me and my brothers were only youngsters when we was taken in by different families here in Fortune Harbour after our father drowned. They gave us the name Hynes. My father was Angelo Haas from up on the French Shore. His father was Jean François Haas from Austria. He jumped off a ship with a French woman from Paris up on the French Shore somewhere around La Scie. It was called François Cove, later called Frenchman's Cove.

They fished up there and had a family and premises. She was supposed to be the best hand at splittin' fish on the French Shore and they said she always wanted a bottle of brandy or rum on the splittin' table while she was at it or she wouldn't split the fish. So it's the two of them we all come from, an Austrian man and a French woman. I was raised by the Irish here in Fortune Harbour and glad to be helped out the way I was by old Tommy Croke. I don't mind being called Hynes but I don't say there's much Irish in me. We are a stocky, strappy crowd, strong as oxes most of us, dogs to work, and we likes our drink and smoke. Perhaps we got that from grandmother, the French Woman from Paris. Is there any beer left in that box?"

Towards the end of that wonderfully calm and sunny summer, Leo and I had landed on headlands and small islands where few people, certainly no geologists, had ever landed before. I had discovered some new aspects of the geology, which could form the basis of my master's thesis, and I had shared many wonderful moments with Hynes family members, as well as the striking miners, over a lot of fish, cigarettes and beer. I wanted to stay forever, but one day in late August Skipper Lou turned to me and said, "Now I think it's soon time to get off the water. The west and nor'west winds are on the way and it won't be fit to go out through the Shoal Tickle after that."

I said my goodbyes to Lou, Helen, Elizabeth, Leo and Lons and all the Hynes family members and the Buchans miners and returned to St. John's and university life where I met up with a Girlologist from Toronto. We got married the following year and I tried being a good husband, partner and graduate student. I was not particularly good at any of it.

## 2

After about four years of struggle, strife and hurt, the marriage was over after several attempts at starting again. Wendy moved back to the mainland. I had close friends who convinced me to buy an old house in St. John's the week after the Hibernia offshore oil discovery was first announced. I finished my degree, worked seasonally, drank regularly and loved several women occasionally. My new old house on Coleman's Lane became a temporary refuge for troubled souls who shared my uncertainty, my habits and my occasional misery and heartache.

One winter's night I was in the house alone and went to bed early to catch up on badly needed sleep. I woke in the middle of the night to find Skipper Lou Hynes standing at the foot of my bed. He and his Austrian blue eyes were full of light and directed me to look to his left, where stood the Virgin Mary. Also full of light, She smiled and approached my bed. She tucked me in, cuddled me and I fell back into a deep sleep.

When I awoke the next morning, I knew that I had been blessed. I felt clean, full of light and life, and fundamentally changed by this visit. I had a permanent smile on my face. I knew that I was going to be all right. The season of hurt was over and there is no season for hate. I also knew that I could make something of my life and eventually love again. I started that day and never looked back except to recall the visit of that night, which I can still do whenever I feel the need. I wondered if Lou had actually died that night and had visited me on his way to another world, but inquiries to his family told me that he was still well and still entertaining family and strangers in spite of the tragic loss of his daughter Elizabeth to cancer.

I lost contact with Lou and all the Hynses until last year when I reached Lons, who is the last of them, living now in Fortune

Harbour with his son. He remembered me and invited me to visit, which I did, and still do a couple of times each year. He tells me all his father's stories and many of his own stories of the time he was fishing with his father. Each visit, Lons asks me to tell him again the story of my visit from his father and the Virgin Mary. It does something for both of us.

He also tells me how much he misses his father and how he regrets the way his father was treated in his final years, how he eventually went to the Botwood Hospital and never went back to his own house even in periods of recovery in his failing health. "I wish you could have come to see him then. He would have been some pleased to see you and to know that you had seen the Blessed Virgin Mary and him together in your bedroom. That would have made some difference to him in the end."

"Lons," I say, "I'm afraid that my life has been full of sins of omission. Some are just a lot bigger, that's all. This is one of the big ones."

# OUR FATHER

He was no stranger to death, having barely survived the typhoid fever that claimed his mother and her two sisters when he was a small child and she was still a young woman. He would tell us how a small suit of clothes had been made for his funeral and that he had recovered only because Aunt Charity Baker would sneak pieces of sweet cake to him when she visited because she thought "starving a fever" was no way to save a dying child. Like all of his brothers and sisters, as well as his fifteen first cousins, all suddenly without mothers, he was raised by his father and the older children.

He never went to school because there was no regular teacher then, and he had little inclination when there was one. There was always lots of work to be done and he quickly learned from his father and brothers the skills necessary for making a living and contributing to the family enterprise: lumbering, sawmilling, carpentry, fishing, hunting and the tending of animals, the horses and sheep. In order to earn some cash, he would leave North Harbour for seasonal jobs in the woods of central Newfoundland, cutting pulpwood or filing bucksaws for the other loggers, one of several skills at which he excelled. Later when the war came on, he worked on the construction of military bases at Gander, Stephenville and Argentia. This provided him with some cash for food and clothing, and fuel and supplies for the family sawmill.

Through these activities and his continued hard work he developed into an independent young man, and that served him very well when the new teacher from Hay Cove arrived, charged with reactivating the Anglican School. Father suddenly found the only woman he ever loved. And she loved him, so they announced their marriage and he started building the house I was born in. He had finished the floor by the September wedding date and they had the wedding dance on the planchin'.

Children followed, the first being Lorna, born in February in the same cottage hospital where Father would eventually lie dying. There were no roads to North Harbour then, so he went over to Come By Chance on a horse and slide to bring mother and child home. The five mile harbour was frozen only around the edges, so he had to skim the frozen sea ice around one whole side of the shoreline to get Mother and Lorna home. Everyone was in their windows watching, ready to jump into action if the ice broke under the horse. It held, because Father knew about winter ice and horses and how to get safely home in challenging conditions. But Lorna and the rest of us still talk about that trip whenever we talk about Father.

Two more girls, Rosanne and Madonna (Donnie) came after Lorna, then me, the first boy. After that Mother and Father took a break for a while before starting up again with two more, Brenda and Alex, seven and nine years on.

One evening, when I was about two years old, Father was filling the lamps with kerosene for the night. We were both outside the door. He went back inside to get a cloth to clean a flue and I downed a pint of the kerosene while he was gone. The nearest doctor or nurse was at Come By Chance and there was no way to get me there in time for any medical response. Father kept me awake all night, afraid that I might not wake up again if I went to sleep. When old Doctor Coxon arrived two days later, he said "You did the right thing. There might have been brain damage if the child had slept. It will pass through him in a few days. Just don't light any matches around him, to be safe."

It was later in my university years that my doctors discovered mysterious scar tissue on my lungs and the related bronchitis whenever I develop a chest cold. Maybe there *was* some brain damage and I'm just now discovering it, in combination with the result of my continued drinking habits as I approach the age my father was when he died.

Father's favourite place in the house was the daybed in the kitchen. He was always up before us to put the fire in the kitchen range, the only source of heat in the house when we were youngsters. He would make a cup of live tea when the stove got hot enough to boil a kettle and would take a spell on the daybed before the rest of us got up and came downstairs to the warm kitchen. When my older sisters became teenagers, they were sometimes slow to get out of bed after nights of dancing parties. Father would turn on the kitchen radio and try to find some latest hit song which might get them awake and up. Once he turned it up loud and bawled up the stairs, "Get up girls! Albert Presley is down here with the world all shook up!"

There were always children in the house, often sharing the daybed with Father and telling one or the other to "Move over on your edge, and make room!" During one of her remodeling efforts, Mother once made the mistake of moving the daybed out of the kitchen and into the shed. Father was not pleased. He moved it back in and said, "Now, Mrs. Dean, leave that where it is." But he usually catered to her whims on rearranging walls and furniture, only commenting when she offered specific directions or advice on how best to go about achieving the desired result; "Now Mrs. Dean," he'd say, "who is doing this job, me or you?" Otherwise, there was never a harsh word spoken, never a voice raised, never an angry thought expressed. Even after he bought a car and Mother had forgotten to take any cash on one of their Sunday or weekend outings, he would just turn around, head back to the house and calmly tell her to go in and get every jeezly dollar she could find.

But he was not really fond of travel or outings, except to visit old friends or relatives for a yarn on a Sunday drive. He was rooted in North Harbour, where he belonged. He left Newfoundland only once in his life. That was when Mother convinced him to go with her and my sister Rosanne and her family to Prince Edward Island. She and the girls had read all the L.M. Montgomery books and dearly wanted to visit the Anne of Green Gables homestead near Cavendish. Mother even bought a swimming suit for herself and a pair of bathing shorts for Father—the first and only pair he ever wore. After several days of touring the Anne of Green Gables sites, where Anne did this and Rilla said that, Father spoke up and declared that Lucy Maud might have had a pee right over there by that big tree. Mother figured it might be a good time to put on the bathing suits and go to Cavendish Beach.

They had come out of the fog of Placentia Bay, untanned for years, if they ever had been. As they passed through a narrow opening in a sand dune, they brushed by a black man in very short shorts who was just leaving the beach. They were barely out of earshot when Mother said, "Oh my! I think that's the blackest man I've ever seen!" "You know what he is thinking?" Father said. "He is thinking that's the whitest woman I ever laid eyes on!"

After that, in spite of Mother's efforts to get him to travel with her to visit her brothers in Toronto, he stayed home in North Harbour. "I thought we might fly up," she would say. To which he would reply, "Are you any good to fly?"

When, under the provincial government resettlement program, families started moving into North Harbour from the islands and more isolated communities of Placentia Bay, Father was both interested and concerned. Seeing people shift their houses was not new for him, but the movement of so many at once from distant places was novel for everyone. He was so rooted in his own place in the Harbour that he knew people could be very fragile when uprooted in this very strange way. He knew they would need warm welcomes and friendly faces and helping hands. He would reach out to them in the best way he could.

He started with the first families, the Upshalls from Harbour Buffett, the Haineses from Tack's Beach, the Slades from Kingwell, and then moved on to the crowd from Port Anne, the Hobens, the Pardys, the Pevies and the Hodders. They all came from places with few roads or little electricity and many had floated their houses down the bay to North Harbour. Father got to know them all. First he offered to wire their houses for electricity, then he gave them lumber, cement, tools: whatever he had that they needed. These new families settled on the far side of Goose Cove, furthest from the shops, the school and the Anglican Church. They had no means of transportation other than the fishing boats they brought with them, so he took them everywhere in his car whenever they needed a ride. Just about every Sunday, Mrs. Hoben or Mrs. Pevie would ask, "Mr. Dean, would you land me over to church?" He always did. He said he wore out a car doing so, because he also landed them back again after church. He was their friend in need, "doing unto others."

When Father turned sixty-five, we had a big family celebration in the community hall in North Harbour. Mother organized the whole event and everybody came: all six of us, the four sons-in-law, most of his nine grandchildren, many nieces and nephews and all his close friends in North Harbour. It was a grand time! We had a great dance and most of us were able to express in some subtle way how happy we were to be all together in one place to celebrate with him and quietly to acknowledge his continued impact on our lives. After the toasts and the words of welcome and celebration, he gave a rare brief speech, concluding with words borrowed from a song by Jim Payne: "Now its wave over wave, sea over bow, I'm as happy a man as sixty-five will allow." He never spoke truer words. He had just spent the past ten years in joyful retirement, at home with Mother, fishing in his own boat and enjoying life with his friends, family and grandchildren.

Before his next birthday, he fell victim to the Dean genes, the various heart and blood ailments that claimed his father and five brothers: he suffered a stroke. After a few months of what seemed like slow improvement, his condition became more complex and he was sent to the Health Sciences hospital in St. John's. There he suffered several months of tests and probing at the whims of several new doctors, but showed no improvement. Finally, he was transferred to the old cottage hospital at Come by Chance, nearer home.

We all took this as a signal that he was unlikely to get any better and that maybe it was just a matter of time. With each visit to his bedside, it seemed clear that he had also come to this conclusion and wanted that time to be shorter rather than longer. The nurses reluctantly informed us that he would try to pull the intravenous tubes from his arms at night and that they had to put oven mitts on his hands to prevent him from injuring himself. He had also lost the ability to speak.

There seemed to be little way of giving comfort to our father in that state, no way to know what to offer beyond moistening his lips with a damp cloth or Q Tip, which might have been as much for us as for him. We all found it particularly frustrating to be unable to provide some help or comfort to the one who had so capably and gracefully given so much help and comfort to so many of his family and friends in time of need or sorrow. He only seemed to brighten somewhat during the visits from Reverend Sam Jones, the Anglican minister from Labrador who was assigned to our parish. Reverend Jones was of Father's age and generation and had also grown up in the "hard times" when work and making a living meant using the strength of your body as well as your brain. Mr. Jones seemed to get through to him, to reach out with some comfort when the rest of us could not. Their connection seemed to become stronger and more important to both of them with each succeeding visit.

The resettled people were all as concerned as we were when Father had the stroke. When he finally succumbed to congestive heart failure in Come By Chance Hospital, at the age of sixty-six, these families mourned the loss with us. They landed up in our house with food and drink. Some, like Henry Pevie, were too sad to actually come inside. He stayed out, just repeating "That Man, that Man. All he done for us!"

In North Harbour, as elsewhere, death brings a series of tasks and decisions. These provide a way for most people, especially family members, to deal with the grief of sudden loss. So, with the help of these needs, we got on with it, just as Father would have done had the deceased been one of us, just as he had done for others many times before. Mother chose the gravesite. "In there next to Mrs.

Hoben, overlooking the bottom of the Harbour." She picked out the hymns to be sung and the gospel passages to be read. His four sons-in-law agreed to serve as pallbearers. Reverend Jones agreed with everything. The church was cleaned and dusted. Digging of the grave was attended to. I was sent to the funeral home to choose an appropriate casket. My sisters provided a continuous stream of tea, food, hugs, smiles, conversation and drink for all arriving visitors and extended family, then prepared for more of the same.

Father was waked in the church he had helped build and then helped move from just outside his own fence to Goose Cove Marsh, closer to the Anglican families who had shifted in from out the Bay. They all came. Everyone came. People we all knew and people we did not know came: contractors, highway workers, shopkeepers, merchants he had provided with lumber and ice, people he had built houses for, people he had rescued from cars drifted in by blizzards on the Burin highway and who had believed they would freeze to death, people he had comforted in their times of hardship and loss, including Mother's sisters and their families. As was their intention and desire, this sharing helped us all.

My sisters asked me to participate in the funeral service, to do one of the readings and perhaps say a word of thanks for all the support and comfort from everybody. I was assigned the piece from First Corinthians 13, which begins, "Though I speak with the tongues of men and angels, and have not charity, I am become as sounding brass, or a tinkling cymbal." It ends with, "And now abideth faith, hope, charity, these three; but the greatest of these is charity." We all felt that this was appropriate for Father. I also selected Tennyson's "Crossing the Bar," a poem I thought might reflect Father's attitude towards his passing from this world.

We all noticed that the Reverend Jones was having difficulty controlling his grief. He was openly weeping at the altar during parts of the Anglican Service for the Burial of the Dead. Mother was her stoic self, sitting next to us in the front pew. She nodded to me when it was time for my reading. I slowly rose to the altar. Calmly and clearly, I read the words of Paul— "The greatest of these is charity"— followed by Tennyson's "One clear call for me." I thanked the whole Harbour for their support and sharing of our grief. "We know that our loss is also your loss. May his spirit live on in North Harbour as he will live on through us, his children and grandchildren."

The day gave comfort and peace. On this day, for a few moments, I was not only my father's son. I was my father.

I go back now to visit the grave where he lies next to Mother and Mrs. Hoben, looking over the bottom of North Harbour, knowing they have been landed in the same place and hoping that he saw his Pilot face to face.

And I always walk away, shaking my head. "Sixty-six, Father," I say. "Sixty-six! You were that young! Sure, I'll soon be that age myself. And there is so much that I still haven't done, "for us.""

# ACKNOWLEDGEMENTS

All of these stories were written for and read at The March Hare literary festival. Thanks to Al Pittman for inviting and encouraging the writing of my first story and to Rex Brown for the annual invitation to read at the Hare and for his constant encouragement and support. Thanks to the many March Hare audiences who listened, applauded and gave important responses over the years. I am very grateful for words of encouragement offered at several March Hare readings by Anita Best, Michael Crummey, Paul Durcan, Stan Dragland, Alistair MacLeod, Lisa Moore and Des Walsh.

Some of the stories are based on events and persons from North Harbour, Placentia Bay, where I was born and raised. Many of these people have now passed on. As told here, some of the events involving them really happened, but my imagination did often grow active as I recalled their characters during the writing of this or that story. They were and still are very real and wonderful to me. Out of respect, and with no intention of offending any person or their memory, I have used their real names in these stories.

An earlier version of "Melvin" appeared in the *March Hare Anthology*, edited by Adrian Fowler (Breakwater Books, 2007). A version of "'Tis Not for the 'Gard of the 'Cardeen" was published in the *Newfoundland Quarterly*, 2003.

I thank Beth Follett of Pedlar Press for kindly and bravely offering to transform a scattered collection of stories, written over many years for a small audience, into a volume that may be read by any who choose to do so. This would not have happened without her and I am deeply grateful. Stan Dragland has been a superb editor for these stories. He has made very important suggestions for improvements to the text.

The stories (and the song) were written to be read aloud (or sung) before a live audience. It is my sincere hope that they may give some joy, laughter or tears to the readers, without hearing my wavering voice.

September 29, 2015

Paul Dean is a geologist, a writer, storyteller and singer from Newfoundland. For fifteen years, he has been a regular performer and reader at The March Hare literary festival, at various locations in Newfoundland and Canada. Many of his stories are based in the small community of North Harbour, Placentia Bay, where he was born and spent his early years. He now lives in St. John's and Trinity East, with his family and many friends.